my LiTTLE PONY™

For my three 'mane' girls – Rachel, Pam and Sidnie

ORCHARD BOOKS
Carmelite House
50 Victoria Embankment
London EC4Y 0DZ

First published in 2013 in the United States
by Little, Brown and Company

This edition published by Orchard Books in 2014

A CIP catalogue record for this book is available
from the British Library.

ISBN 978 1 40833 123 1

11

Printed in Great Britain by CPI Group (UK) Ltd, Croydon, CR0 4YY

Orchard Books
Am imprint of Hachette Children's Group
Part of The Watts Publishing Group Limited
An Harchette UK Company
www.hachette.co.uk

Twilight Sparkle

* * and * *

The Crystal Heart Spell

Written by G. M. Berrow

ORCHARD

Contents
★ ★ ★

Chapter 1

A Crown Achievement

All of Equestria had been celebrating since the joyous wedding of Shining Armour and Princess Mi Amore Cadenza – or Cadance, as she was called. The citizens of Equestria, including the newly recovered Crystal Empire, were living in a time of happiness and prosperity. Apples grew in the orchards, creatures big and small played in the lush green fields, and ponies of all three tribes lived in harmony. And now, another promising young royal had joined the highest ranks of pony society. It seemed like the cherry on top of a delicious ice-cream sundae.

Ponies of all kinds from the far reaches of Princess Celestia's kingdom were curious about the new princess who had just been crowned. She was a young Unicorn pony with a violet-hued hide, a beautiful purple-and-pink striped mane, and incredible abilities. Her name was Twilight Sparkle, and she was indeed very special. Stories of her amazing magical gifts had travelled all the way from San Franciscolt to Manehattan. These tales had started to become legendary – especially the one about the time she defeated the evil Queen Chrysalis in order to save the royal court of Canterlot. All the ponies in Equestria were excited to see what wonders Twilight Sparkle's reign would bring.

Twilight was excited too. Not only did she bear an esteemed new title, but she had received her very own set of wings. *Real* Pegasus wings! She was officially part of a special breed of pony called an Alicorn. This meant that Twilight was now able to harness the magical powers of the Unicorns, the flight abilities of the Pegasi, and the strength of a good, true heart of an Earth Pony. She was becoming more like her teacher, the talented and kind Princess Celestia, every day.

Although it was very exciting for Twilight to become an Alicorn, she didn't take her new gifts for granted. It was an honour to be part of something so rare. She didn't care about all the shiny jewels and castle rooms she'd been given. She was happy to remain in Ponyville for now. She loved to spend time in her library with Spike, the baby dragon who was her number-one assistant, and having barrels of fun with her best friends.

Ever since Princess Celestia had sent Twilight away from Canterlot to study and learn the magic of friendship, she had felt that Ponyville was her true home. Twilight was uncertain how she would feel if she had to leave – let alone rule a kingdom.

It was true that Twilight Sparkle loved to help other ponies, to teach them the interesting facts she'd read about in the pages of her beloved books. She also enjoyed her position as leader of the Ponyville Winter Wrap-Up. But being in charge of a kingdom of ponies didn't seem easy. Twilight was nervous. She still had so much to learn. But, then again, there was *always* more to learn. The world was so vast and fascinating!

✳ ✳ ✳

One afternoon in Ponyville, just after the Pegasi had moved some clouds into the sky for a short rainfall, Twilight went home to scour every book in her library yet again. She was hoping for some guidance on exactly how a pony could become a great princess and leader.

There was bound to be some information in one of her books that could help her.

She thought she was on to something when she first laid a hoof on the pages of *The Princess Bridle*. It was one of her favourite stories about royal ponies, but not quite right.

"What about this one, Twi?" Spike said, pulling a dusty book from one of the low shelves. He couldn't reach the higher ones without a ladder. The book was titled *Purple Reign* by Crystal Ball. But that was no good either. It just had lots of song lyrics in it.

"Spike!" Twilight exclaimed. "What am I going to do?" She threw her hoof up into the air. "I need some help. I just know there's more to being a leader than what I already know." Twilight began to pace the room in her usual manner. She did this so often that the floorboards had worn down, forming a large circle. Spike liked to call it the Twilight Zone.

Spike furrowed his scaly brow and clapped his claws together. "That's it!" He sprang up and knocked several titles from the shelf. A moment later, he appeared in the pile of fallen books, clutching one with a familiar blue-and-yellow cover. Twilight recognised it immediately as *Daring Do and the Trek to the Terrifying Tower*. She had already read all the books in the series about the fearless pony adventurer at least three times.

Twilight cocked her head to the side. "I don't get it, Spike. What's Daring Do got to 'do' with it?"

"Well, you know how Daring has to rescue a pony who's been locked in a tower surrounded by a moat filled with sharp-toothed piranhas?"

"Yeah...so?"

"And you know how she has to dive into the water to reach the tower, even though fish are secretly her biggest fear?"

"Spike! Spit it out!" Twilight exclaimed. "Do you have an idea of how to help me or not?" She was beginning to look a bit stressed. Her mane had gone frizzy and one of her eyes was twitching ever so slightly. Twilight took her responsibilities very seriously – sometimes too seriously.

"Well, basically Daring Do wants to overcome her fears once and for all. So she asks some older ex-adventurer ponies, like Professor A. B. Ravenhoof, for tips on how to do it!" Spike spread his short arms wide in triumph.

Aha! It was so obvious to Twilight now. She needed guidance from someone wiser. "Why didn't *I* think of that?" Twilight's face lit up, thinking of all the ponies she could interview. "Good work, Spike! It's perfect." Spike blushed. He loved nothing more than to be a good assistant to his best friend. But he could hardly say "You're welcome!" before Twilight Sparkle was out of the door to find out about the great leaders of Equestria – straight from the horses' mouths.

CHAPTER 2

A Foal House

"Who in Ponyville might be able to help me?" Twilight said aloud as she trotted through the town square. She caught sight of Mayor Mare walking on the opposite side of the courtyard, heading into the town hall with a group of important-looking ponies. The mayor ran their whole town! She would definitely know a thing or two about leadership. It was a good place to start.

But by the time she reached the steps of the town hall, the mayor was already behind closed doors. "Sorry, Princess Twilight," Senior Mint, the tall green guard pony said. "Ms Mayor Mare is in a long meeting about next year's Summer Sun Celebration."

Twilight slumped in defeat. "Oh well. But you don't have to call me Princess. Just Twilight will do." Senior Mint nodded, embarrassed.

"Will you tell her I stopped by?" Twilight asked. Maybe they could talk later.

"Yes, of course, Princess Twilight." He cupped a hoof over his mouth. "Oops, I mean *Just Twilight.*"

"Thanks!" She flashed her shiny white smile, turned on her hoof, and headed back to the town square. Suddenly, she smelt the scent of something sweet and scrumptious. Her tummy rumbled.

"Fresh cupcakes! Extra icing!" shouted Carrot Cake, the town baker. He was pulling a pink-and-yellow cart filled with sugary delicacies of every flavour and colour. Maybe it was time for a snack!

"Hello, Mr Cake!" Twilight said, trotting up to the cart, which had begun to draw a crowd of hungry ponies. Twilight hadn't seen such a commotion since the last apple juice sale at Sweet Apple Acres.

"Hi there, Twilight Sparkle!" said Mr Cake.

"Is this your new treat cart?" she asked. "What a wonderful idea!"

"Mrs Cake and I are always trying to come up with new ways to share our desserts with the ponies of Ponyville." Pumpkin Cake and Pound Cake, twin foals, giggled and trotted alongside their father. Pound Cake, who was a Pegasus, beat his little wings until he was hovering near a tray of pink and purple pastries. When his father wasn't watching, he sneakily snatched one and ate it in a single greedy bite. His sister, Pumpkin Cake, jumped as high as she could to grab one, but she couldn't quite reach. She finally used her Unicorn magic to steal a blue cupcake and deliver it gently to her mouth. She licked her lips. Then she burped.

"Plus, the babies love to get out of the shop," Mr Cake continued, too busy to notice his little foals' naughty actions. "Fresh air does them good!"

Twilight watched as Pumpkin and Pound chased each other in circles and through the legs of a nearby grey Pegasus pony. The pony wobbled helplessly before toppling over into a nearby rosebush. When she popped her head out, her lemon-yellow mane was adorned with prickly thorns. "Mr Cake! Do you have any muffins today?" she called. Her hoof got caught on a branch, and she tumbled onto the soft grass.

"Fresh out of muffins, unfortunately,"

Carrot replied, looking concerned.

"Well, *I'll* take one cupcake, please." Twilight licked her lips. Mr Cake reached inside the glass display case, but all that was left were crumbs. "Oh dear, we seem to be out of *everything*!" He frowned.

"Why don't you trot back to SugarCube Corner with us?" Carrot offered. "Mrs Cake is sure to have whipped up some more by now."

Twilight hesitated. She was supposed to be on a fact-finding mission, not eating cakes. Her stomach rumbled again and Pumpkin Cake giggled.

"I guess that's my answer," Twilight said. "Just for a few minutes, though. Then I have to get back to my quest."

The twins cheered and hopped on Twilight's back for a ride to the bakery. "Giddyup!" they chorused.

"Mrs Cake, this rainbow chip... *mmmf*... delight is... delicious," Twilight said with a full mouth. A dollop of pink icing made its way down her chin. "Excuse me," she said as she cleaned her face. "I don't mean to eat and run like this, but I really must go."

"Of course, Princess," Mrs Cake said, bowing quickly. She continued to pipe a tube of icing onto a strawberry-layer cake, creating a beautiful border of plump roses.

Twilight blushed. "You really don't have to call me that," she replied. This *princess* business was tricky. Maybe she should put up a banner in the town square telling everyone to treat her as they normally would. "I'm just the same old Twilight, really."

She caught sight of her reflection in the shiny cake display case. Other than the new wings, she still looked the same. She wasn't even wearing her tiara. "In fact, I don't really know how to be a princess at all. That's what I'm doing today. I'm trying to ask some older ponies what it means to be a leader, but I don't want to ask Princess Celestia – that would be embarrassing – and when I tried to see Mayor Mare, she was busy and…" Everything spilled out at once.

Mrs Cake furrowed her brow in motherly concern. "My goodness, that sounds like a sticky situation. Why don't you visit your big brother and Princess Cadance?"

Twilight smiled. What a great idea!

Her BBBFF (Big Brother Best Friend For Ever) Shining Armour and new Pegasister-in-law had much more royal experience than she did. "You're a genius! They are bound to have some royal advice!"

Carrot Cake popped his head in from the storeroom. "We're not out of royal icing! We have a whole carriage full back here, my dear!"

"No, Carrot," Mrs Cake shouted back. "Royal *advice*. For Twilight!"

She shook her head, sighing. "Stallions. They never listen."

Twilight chuckled as she made her way out of the door. "Maybe I'd better talk to Cadance and *not* Shining Armour." She was feeling more confident now that she had a real plan. "Thanks for the terrific tips and treats, Mrs Cake! Bye, Pumpkin! Bye, Pound!" And then the young monarch was off to find out exactly what made a royal pony tick.

CHAPTER 3

Empire State of Mind

Twilight Sparkle didn't think it was possible, but the Crystal Empire looked even more beautiful than the last time she'd been there. The winding, cobble-gem streets and tall spires sparkled in the sunshine. It had been a long journey, but it was well worth it to be back.

Everything appeared to be fully restored to its former glory, partly thanks to her, of course, though she would never brag about it. The Crystal Empire had been through many dark days after the evil King Sombra tried to keep the source of the Empire's power – the Crystal Heart – hidden away. The Crystal Heart, charged by the power of the ponies' love, was the only object that was able to offer the Empire protection. Once it was stolen, the kingdom was overtaken by darkness.

Luckily, Princess Celestia had put Twilight to the test when she recruited her and her friends to help. They came to the rescue, putting on the long-forgotten Crystal Faire while Twilight searched for the Crystal Heart. When Twilight finally succeeded in recovering the precious, magical gemstone, not only did she pass her test, but balance was also restored to the city.

As Twilight walked past a group of Crystal ponies, she smiled and waved. "Good afternoon, everyone!"

"Hey, Princess Twilight Sparkle!" they shouted in response. "Welcome back!"

A sparkling teal-coloured pony with a light blue mane jumped up and down in excitement. The pony was named Glitter Dance and reminded Twilight of her eternally energetic friend, Pinkie Pie. "We're going to the Crystal Lake today!" she exclaimed. "Come and play with us!"

Twilight politely declined but was pleased with the invitation. The ponies were having tons of fun with one another, which was always a good sign. Every corner of the kingdom appeared to be filled with light and love. It was certainly the perfect place for Shining Armour and Princess Cadance to live and rule.

"Twily!" a handsome white stallion with a blue mane yelled from across the courtyard. Shining Armour hadn't seen his sister since her coronation. He galloped over and embraced her in a classic big-brother hug. "How's my second-favourite princess?" He knocked her cheek lovingly with his hoof.

"Hey, now!" Twilight laughed. "I was around first!"

"Only kidding!" he said as Princess Cadance trotted over to join them.

"You're *both* my favourite princesses."

"Cadance!" Twilight called out.
"*Sunshine...sunshine...*" she started,
looking to the elegant princess for
acknowledgment.

"*Ladybirds awake!*" Cadance yelled in
joyous response.

The two of them sang in unison as
they hopped around and shook their tails
at each other. "*Clap your hooves and do
a little shake!*" It had been their secret
tailshake since Twilight was just a little
filly and Cadance was her foal-sitter.
It was still amusing after all these years,
even though a couple of nearby ponies
watched the scene in confusion. It was
unusual to see their princess acting
so silly.

"So what brings you to the Crystal
Empire, little sis?" Shining Armour

asked. "Isn't royal life great?" He beamed with pride and smiled wide. His little sister had come so far in her studies that she'd achieved princess status.

"Well... that's sort of why I'm here." Twilight dropped her eyes to the ground and scuffed a hoof around. "I don't know how to act! I don't feel anything like a princess, and it's weird to have everyone call me that. I don't feel very graceful... Not like you, Cadance."

"Oh, Twilight!" said Shining Armour. "It isn't easy. But you're doing great!"

Twilight knew he was trying to help, but she couldn't resist rolling her eyes a little bit. "Of course you would say that. You're my brother – you have to think so!"

"Chill out, Twily. Being royalty is easy! Right, Cadance?"

Cadance's face became serious. "No,

Shining Armour. It's not as simple as that. I completely understand what she's going through." She turned to her fellow princess. "Maybe I can help you, Twilight."

She started by leading Twilight Sparkle down the street and through the city. Twilight was happy to follow.

Chapter 4

A Tail to Tell

It was a busy day in the Crystal Empire. The streets were bustling with Crystal ponies rushing home from the markets and shops, their packs filled with fresh apples and other luxuries.

"Good afternoon, Moondust!" Cadance greeted an iridescent white pony with a sleek silver mane. She was selling baskets of Crystal berries at a little stand near the fountain. "How are your foals?"

The pony beamed as she bowed to the two princesses. "They are wonderful! Would you like some fresh Crystal berries?" Moondust asked, and gave them each a small bunch. The sweet tartness exploded in Twilight's mouth as she devoured them. Twilight made a mental note to bring some back for the Cakes. The berries would taste delicious in a pie.

"Thank you very much!" Twilight said as they walked away. How did Cadance do that – remember the names of a whole kingdom's residents? Twilight sometimes found it difficult to remember the names of just the entire Apple family.

"I always try to remember every pony in the kingdom, because each one is special," Cadance explained as they walked. "We all play our part in making the kingdom a happy and fun place to live."

Twilight sighed. Cadance definitely had a point, but all these new responsibilities were starting to add up.

"You're such a great princess, Cadance," Twilight said. "I wish I could be like you. I feel so lost."

"I didn't always feel so confident," Cadance said.

"You didn't?" Twilight asked, trying to think of a time when Cadance had seemed as lost as she felt now.

"When I was found as a baby Pegasus, in a forest far, far away..." Cadance began the familiar tale. Twilight listened intently as Cadance recounted her path to becoming the great pony leader she was today.

Cadance told her how
some Earth Ponies
from a nearby
village took
her in as
their own
little filly.
And as she
grew up, the natural love and compassion
she had for others filled everyone with
warmth and the urge to protect her.

But all was not well for long.

An evil pony enchantress named
Prismia lived alone nearby. She rarely
came out of her cottage because she felt
nothing but jealousy for the other ponies
in the village – the way they loved and
took care of one another. And yet, she
had no one who cared for her. Prismia

wore a powerful necklace, which she cared for more than anything else in the world, and it served to amplify the evil and jealousy within her own heart. When Prismia's bad feelings and the power of the necklace finally overtook her, she cast a spell on the villagers that leeched all the love from their homes. She hoped to capture some of that love for herself.

Cadance decided that she couldn't let that happen, so she went to see Prismia. Luckily, the enchantress's powerful necklace also amplified the power of Cadance's love, and she soon defeated Prismia with her incredible kindness. Once Prismia changed her horrible ways, Cadance was surrounded by magical energy and transported to a strange place – a place that no one except Princess Celestia had ever been! So when Celestia discovered Cadance in that mysterious location, her fate was sealed. The princess brought her back to Canterlot to raise her as her very own royal niece – the special young Princess Cadance.

Princess Cadance's talent had always been her ability to spread love wherever she went – settling conflicts and bringing ponies together. In her final exam at Celestia's school of magic, Cadance was even able to make two known rival pony families of Canterlot become best friends for life.

"So I spent a long time in Canterlot just resolving conflicts and helping other ponies find love. I never really experienced it for myself." Cadance giggled. "Even though I *did* have a crush on your brother."

Twilight made a disgusted face. "Yuck."

"Everyone was telling me what a great princess I would be someday, but I just didn't feel like I knew what to do!" Cadance said. Twilight nodded in enthusiastic agreement. Now they were talking. "So I went to Princess Celestia for advice."

"And...?" Twilight asked, all ears.

"She asked me if I *felt* like a true leader." Cadance turned to her young companion. "I told her that no, sadly, I didn't."

"And...?" Twilight repeated. She could hardly take the suspense!

Cadance continued, "She told me about an ancient spell that had the power to make anyone who was destined to lead become the pony they were meant to be."

Twilight smiled. She *knew* that there was an answer to all of this – and of course it was a spell!

True leadership was only an enchantment away.

★ ★ ★

The two ponies soon found themselves standing in front of a giant crystal statue of Cadance. The sun shone through it, creating hundreds of tiny rainbows in the water flowing through the fountain. "Wow, they must really love you here, Cadance." Twilight could never imagine having a statue of herself. It was a bit much.

Cadance shook her head and shrugged. "Oh, I guess so!" she said, chuckling.

The famous, powerful Crystal Heart

stood next to the statue, shining brilliantly with the magic of the Crystal ponies. Thankfully, it was safely displayed right where Twilight had last left it, rather than hidden away with some evil king. Rescuing the heart once had been difficult enough. She didn't want to have to do it again.

"So where can I find this leader spell, then? Can you teach it to me? Is it in one of the old spell books?" Twilight asked eagerly. As soon as she learned the words from Cadance, she'd be on her way back to Ponyville. Then everything would be solved.

"Oh, no, Twilight." Cadance shook her head. "This spell isn't something that can just be learned. The Crystal Heart Spell can only be revealed when a future leader of Equestria understands what her biggest challenge in leadership will be. Only then will she know how to rule, in her heart."

Twilight furrowed her brow in confusion. What in Equestria was Cadance talking about? *Revealed?* Twilight was somehow supposed to get some random spell to appear out of thin air? This was going to be trickier than she'd expected.

"How am I supposed to do that?!"

"I can help you with one clue, just as Celestia did with me." Cadance's voice was gentle and reassuring. "Just think about the elements that make up a great kingdom, Twilight."

"The Elements of Harmony?" Twilight asked. It was the first thing that popped into her mind, so it probably was too obvious.

"Not exactly..." Cadance said. "What

are the best things we have in Equestria?"

Twilight looked completely baffled.
Cadance thought it might be time for a
different approach. So she began to
recount her search for the spell in greater
depth. Cadance warned Twilight, though,
that the spell worked differently for every
pony. It couldn't be repeated.

"Once I received the clue myself, I
decided to start by asking my friends what
they thought," Cadance remembered.
"They had all sorts of crazy ideas about
what they liked in a kingdom."

"Like what?"

"Well, my friend Buttercream said she
thought every kingdom should have a
chocolate fountain in the centre. And
another pony I knew, Sky Chariot,
suggested a curfew time for all ponies to
be home by." Cadance scrunched up

her face in distaste. "I didn't really agree with any of them, but I used their ideas anyway."

Twilight nodded along as she listened to the story.

"But nothing happened!" Cadance said dramatically. "The spell was nowhere to be found, and I was more lost than ever."

Twilight's eyes grew wide. "So how did you find it?"

"One day, I was sitting by the lake just outside Canterlot," Cadance recalled. "I thought about how all I had ever done was listen to the suggestions or commands of other ponies."

"Like the way they would always ask you to help them fall in love?" Twilight asked.

"Yes, exactly! I never made any

decisions for myself." Cadance stared out into the water of the crystal fountain. "As soon as I realised this, the spell appeared, shimmering in gold letters on the surface of the lake."

"Wow…" Twilight cooed, imagining the pretty scene.

"As I read the spell aloud, I instantly knew that my destiny was to lead other ponies with my strengths of True Love and Tolerance. But the only way to do it was by listening to my *own* heart as well."

CHAPTER 5

A Gift Horse

Cadance led Twilight through a wooden
door and into a castle bedroom. It was
decked out in rich, royal velvets of deep
purple and gold. Precious gems of every
colour adorned the bed frame and hung
from the chandelier. The early evening
light shining through tall windows onto

the lavish furnishings was dazzling.

Twilight blinked in disbelief. "This room is all mine?"

"Well, not *all* yours!" Spike popped out from behind the purple curtains and did a dance. "Surprise!" Cadance laughed at the little dragon's antics.

"Spike!" Twilight instantly felt guilty for leaving him behind. "Sorry I left Ponyville in such a rush."

"It's just lucky you came back here when you did," said Spike. "I almost ate that bed while I was waiting." Spike's eyes grew large as he looked around. Jewels and crystals were his favourite meal. It had taken a lot of self-control to keep him from nibbling the furniture.

"Good thing you didn't." Twilight's

eyes landed on a small, wrapped golden box that was sitting on the bed. "Spike, you didn't have to bring me a present. It's not my birthday!"

"But I didn't…" said Spike.

"It's from me," explained Cadance, nudging it towards Twilight with her muzzle. "Just a little gift from one princess to another."

Twilight tore open the packaging. Inside was a beautiful necklace made of purple jewels. At the centre was a large gem in the shape of a heart. It had a quality to it that Twilight had seen only one other place…

"Cadance, is this your favourite necklace? From when we were growing up?" As a filly, Twilight had admired the necklace. It had always seemed to be extra special in some way that she couldn't quite put her hoof on.

Cadance smiled warmly. "Of course it is! I think it's time that a new princess wore it proudly."

"Oh, Cadance!" Twilight put the necklace on and spun around. "I'll take such good care of it! Thank you."

"Of course, my dear new sister," Cadance said as she made her way to the door. "I just want you to know one thing."

Twilight was spinning around in front of the mirror, dreamy-eyed. "Yes?" she said.

"The rare gem in the middle has been enchanted with a powerful charm," Cadance explained. "As long as the pony wearing it is filled with the magic of love and positivity, the necklace will wrap her in warmth and protection."

"It sounds amazing!" Twilight said.

"Wait, is this the same necklace from the story? That Prismia wore?"

"It very well may be," said Cadance with a wink before she turned serious again. "But you must also remember that if the pony wearing it does *not* display love and positivity, it will only magnify her negative thoughts! Be careful, Twilight. If you stay true to your heart, the spell will soon reveal itself." And with that, Cadance was gone.

"Got it," Twilight replied lazily, exhaustion from the long journey finally overtaking her. She climbed into the comfy bed and nuzzled down under the covers. In the morning, she would begin to look for the elements of a perfect kingdom. "True to your heart…" she whispered before falling into a sweet, dreamless slumber.

She'd only been there a day, but Twilight
Sparkle's Crystal Suite was already a mess.
All the books from the shelf in the room
were pulled out, littering the floor and
bed. Some were open at pages filled with
spells and history lessons; others lay
closed in stacks. Spike sat on the window
seat, gazing out at the panoramic view
of the Crystal Empire and then looking
closer with a telescope. He was trying
to guess how many crystals were out
there and also how yummy each one
would taste.

"Where did Cadance say she started
looking for the spell?" Twilight asked
Spike, who hopped down and started
restacking the books.

"I don't know!" Spike replied. "I was up here waiting for you, remember? I didn't hear her story."

Twilight picked up the box that held her gorgeous new necklace. As soon as she slipped it on and looked in the mirror, she knew exactly what to do. "She asked her friends for their opinions – that's what Cadance did!" Twilight exclaimed. "Spike, take down a letter! No – make that *five* letters! I'm going to hold a secret spell summit with my best friends."

A meeting of the greatest minds in Ponyville was just what was needed.

Chapter 6

On a Scroll

Spike had been busy all day delivering the invitations for Twilight's emergency secret meeting. He'd visited Fluttershy's cottage first. She accepted and asked Spike if he wanted to come inside and play with her new fruit bat, Toby. "He's so shy, and I think he could use a friend like you,

Spike," she said in her gentle voice.

"Sorry, Fluttershy! I have all these scrolls to deliver. Maybe Toby and I can 'hang out' later!" Spike chuckled at his own joke, but Fluttershy looked confused. "Get it? 'Hang out'? Because bats hang upside down?"

"Oh yes! See you at the meeting!"

Next, he found Applejack working in the orchard at Sweet Apple Acres. She

bucked her hind legs against a tree and a batch of juicy apples came tumbling down into a basket. "A meeting with Twilight?" Applejack looked relieved. "Phew! I haven't seen her for days! I was about to send out the Apple family search party."

"Did someone say *party*?!" An excited Pinkie Pie popped out from behind a tree. "Because my Party Watch just went off!"

She held up her hoof to show Spike and Applejack a bright neon accessory. It looked like a watch, but instead of numbers it just had pictures of colourful balloons, streamers and confetti with the word *party* spelled out twelve times. Little blinking lights rimmed the edge, and a honking noise was being emitted from a tiny speaker at the top.

"But where are all the numbers?"

Applejack asked, confused.

"Who needs numbers?" Pinkie shrugged.

"To see what time it is, silly!" Applejack threw her hooves in the air.

"But it does tell the time! It's party time...all the time!" Pinkie shouted with glee. "Now who said the magic word, huh? Huh?!" She came up to Spike and looked him straight in the eye. "Was it you?"

"It's not a party, really...but here you go, Pinkie." Spike handed her a scroll.

She unfurled it and read the message. "A secret meeting party?! Oh goody! I have to go and get ready!" And Pinkie Pie bounced off towards her house.

"Thanks, Spike," Applejack said, shaking her head. "I guess you can count me and Pinkie in."

Rarity, on the other hand, was less thrilled about the invitation. She peered down at the scroll through her purple cat's-eye work glasses. "I'm in the middle of making a huge order of hornaments! Can this wait until later?" Rarity was always trying to finish some new garment or accessory for her Carousel Boutique.

"Twilight said it was an emergency." Spike looked down at his feet. He didn't want to upset Rarity, because he really liked her. But she always responded to a few well-worded compliments. "Say, Rarity… have you done something special to your mane? It looks super-duper shiny!"

"Well, I did go to the spa this morning to have my hooves done and they used some new conditioner..." Rarity began. Five minutes later, Spike was still standing there. "...and so I said, 'Darling, if you must do my tail as well, just do it.' I knew it would be worth it!"

"Well, it looks great! Gotta run!" Spike quickly said before heading off down the road. He had spent a while listening to chatter about the latest beauty treatments in Ponyville, and now he was running late. Luckily, he had only one stop left. Rainbow Dash was the last pony he had to invite to Twilight's secret meeting.

"Special delivery for one Miss Rainbow Dash!" Spike shouted half-heartedly at the clouds. He was ready to call it a day by the time he reached Ponyville Park. It was directly under Cloudsdale, so there was a good chance of finding the Pegasus there.

"Rainbow Daaaash!" he called out impatiently. "I have a very important invitation to a very secret meeting at Twilight Sparkle's cottage!"

"Hold your ponies, Spike," Rainbow Dash said, swooping down from a cloud. "I'm comin'!"

Rainbow zoomed by a cloud that looked empty, but hidden inside was nosy Gilda the Griffon – and she had heard every word!

Suddenly, the "secret meeting" was not so secret.

✶ ✦ ✶

"So what is this all about, Twi?" Applejack asked as she bit into one of the apple fritters she'd brought for the meeting. All five of Twilight's best friends had turned up, even though they had other things to do. Twilight knew she was lucky that they'd come to help her, no questions asked. It filled Twilight with a sense of pride that made her new necklace shine doubly bright.

Twilight cleared her throat and looked at each of the ponies in the circle. "Thank you all for coming—" she began, and was immediately interrupted by Rarity.

"Is that divine necklace around your neck made of Cosmic Spectrum?" She stared at Twilight's new accessory with desire. "I have only seen pictures of it in books! My, it's gorgeous! It almost looks like a mini version of the Crystal Heart."

Rarity trotted over to get a closer look.

"Thanks! It was a present from Princess Cadance."

"You know what they say about Cosmic Spectrum..." Rarity added, turning to the other ponies. "When you wear it, you must remember—"

"Oh, totally. Yeah, I know all about it," Twilight said in order to keep the meeting moving. She didn't want to listen to Rarity talk about gemstones right now. The clock was ticking! Rarity shrugged, a little hurt. She trotted back to her spot and plopped down.

"*Anyway*, thank you all for coming at such short notice." Twilight looked around at each of her friends with genuine gratitude. "I've asked you here because I desperately need your help—"

"Ooooh! I know!" Pinkie Pie

interrupted with a squeal. "You're planning an undercover jewel-heist mission and you want us all to join 'Sparkle's Six'?"

Twilight shook her head. "Not exactly."

Pinkie Pie was wearing a tan trench coat and a fedora hat in an attempt to disguise herself for the meeting. She had also brought along a drink she called "Secret Punch" as a refreshment, but she wouldn't reveal what the ingredients were, because it was a "super big secret". As a result, no one wanted to drink it. "Or...you volunteered to plan this year's Hearth's Warming Eve pageant and you need us to help?!"

"Pinkie, it's still summertime," Rainbow Dash said, rolling her eyes.

"Whatever it is, can we just get started?" Rarity whined. "I have lots of work to finish! Those hornaments are due in Neigh York by tomorrow morning and they aren't going to finish rhinestoning themselves.

Do you have the time, Pinkie?" Rarity motioned towards Pinkie's Party Watch.

"Sure!" Pinkie said, and looked at her wrist. "It's 'party'."

"Pardon me?" Rarity looked confused. Applejack and Spike couldn't help but giggle, since they knew what was coming. "The time is party?"

"It's party tiiiiime!" Pinkie cheered, and did a skipping lap around the room. Everyone laughed except Rarity, who just looked annoyed.

"Okay, everyone! That's enough," Twilight said. "Down to business."

The ponies listened as Twilight recounted her trip to the Crystal Empire. She told them about Cadance's journey to find the Crystal Heart Spell. Twilight explained that the only way she herself would find it was with her friends' help. Just like Cadance.

"So I'll need you all to come up with some ideas. If you don't, I'll never find the spell and I'll never learn to be a leader and I'll never be a great princess!" Twilight said in one breath.

"Calm down, Twilight," Fluttershy said, patting her on the back. "I'm sure that we can all figure this out together."

"Together?" Twilight asked hopefully. "You'll help me?"

The rest of the ponies nodded and

held up their full cups of Secret Punch in a toast. "Together!"

CHAPTER 7

Brainstorming the Castle

The six ponies had been brainstorming for ever, but Twilight felt like she was even further away from finding the spell than before. The conversation kept going in circles. They all had very different ideas about what they would do if they were in charge.

"There should be an official Cake Day!" Pinkie said, licking her lips. "Every pony in the kingdom just eats cake all day, like a giant birthday party!"

"A royal guard made up of the fastest Pegasus ponies would be awesome," Rainbow Dash chimed in. "We could hold a race to find out who's the best." She pointed to herself. "Other than me, of course."

Twilight took note, but knew this was not the sort of information she was looking for. She sighed. "Applejack? Any ideas?"

Applejack's eyes lit up. "Oooh! How about making everyone have dinner with their families every night like the Apple family does?" she said earnestly. "Strong families build a strong community."

"Okaaay," Twilight said, thinking of her own brother and parents and how far away they lived. It was a nice thought, but it wasn't practical. Not everyone was lucky enough to live near their family.

"I have an idea!" Fluttershy offered.

"You do?" Twilight replied, her ears perking up.

Fluttershy was softly spoken, but she could be very creative.

"I was just thinking how great it would be if there were a place where all the baby animals could play together in safety, far from the scary creatures of the Everfree Forest. Like a

nature reserve, but just for baby animals!
That's what I would do."

"Ummm...okay," Twilight said, and
wrote down the idea.

Twilight was starting to rethink her
plan. She needed real ideas about how a
kingdom works, not silly ones about baby
animals and cakes. "Rarity, any ideas?
You've been awfully quiet over there."

"Well, sure. If you *actually* want my
opinion..." Rarity grumbled. Ever since
she'd tried to warn Twilight about the
necklace and was shut down, Rarity
hadn't felt like saying a peep. "I would
design a fashion line, just for the
kingdom. Exclusive pieces made from
extravagant fabrics so that every pony
would look and feel their best!"

Pinkie Pie and Fluttershy nodded in
excited agreement, but Twilight wasn't

impressed. "Fashions, Rarity?" Twilight shook her head in defeat. "Come on, you guys! Think outside the box!"

"Well, sorry if my idea wasn't good enough for you, *Princess*." Rarity stuck her nose in the air. "I wish you luck in coming up with a better one." Then she trotted out of Twilight's cottage in a huff.

"Whoops," Twilight said, finally realising she had hurt Rarity's feelings. "I didn't mean to make her feel bad. I think I got a little carried away. Sorry, everyone. I guess that's enough for tonight."

CHAPTER 8

Gilda's Got Game

Gilda the Griffon waited patiently outside
Twilight's cottage until the
last pony had left the secret summit.
Pinkie Pie hung around for ages giving
suggestions for different celebrations
to throw.

"Thanks, Pinkie," Twilight said as she

walked her to the door. "I'll certainly consider making Gummy's birthday an official holiday." Gummy was Pinkie Pie's pet alligator.

"Great!" Pinkie squealed. "He'll be so excited when I tell him the news!"

All of a sudden, a crazy noise started sounding from Pinkie's watch. "I've got to go, Twilight! I totally forgot about the housewarming party at Berry Punch's new place!" With that, Pinkie bounced off into the distance.

"Finally! I thought those ponies would never leave," Gilda said, swooping down from a cloud and landing softly in front of Twilight. "Productive meeting, Twilight?"

"Hey! How did you know about the meeting?" Twilight asked suspiciously. It was supposed to be a secret.

"I have my ways," Gilda said, pacing around Twilight. "And I listened to the whole thing. Didn't sound like your friends had *any* good ideas for your kingdom . . ."

"So what, Gilda?" Twilight answered back. "You think you can do better?"

"I'm just trying to say that if *I* were a princess like you, I wouldn't be listening to anyone else's suggestions. I would do whatever I wanted! Make my kingdom all about Gilda!" The griffon cackled and flew off into the clouds again to cause some mischief elsewhere.

Twilight brushed it off. No one in their right mind would take advice from Gilda, the notorious bully. Twilight still trusted her best friends the most. And why shouldn't she? They had proved themselves to be honest and loyal.

But then again, they didn't have years of magical study with Princess Celestia under their belts like Twilight did. And her friends had never even lived in Canterlot, so it was silly to expect them to know very much about being royal.

Twilight went back inside her cottage and looked into a large chest. It was filled with her new gowns and jewels from the coronation. None of it seemed like hers.

 She removed a tiara from its velvet case and placed it gently on her head. In the mirror, the sparkling white diamonds and red rubies shone brilliantly. The tiara made her stand a little taller.

Maybe Gilda had a point. Maybe the secret to leadership was listening to your own heart instead of everyone else's. Isn't that what Cadance had said?

If she was going to be a real princess, maybe she just needed to start acting like one.

$$\star \; \star \; \star$$

The search for the Crystal Heart Spell was beginning to wear on Twilight, even though she was doing her best to try to act like a princess. She still didn't know where or how to look for it!

She even felt like she was hearing voices. For example, that morning in the Ponyville marketplace she'd asked Cheerilee which type of berries she should buy. Cheerilee had suggested the blackberries, but Twilight could've sworn she'd heard a voice coming from a stack of crates saying, "Who cares what *she* likes? What kind of berries do *you* want?"

Later, when Twilight was looking after the Cutie Mark Crusaders – Apple Bloom, Scootaloo and Sweetie Belle – she'd heard it again. They'd all been in Ponyville Park, deciding on an afternoon activity. Twilight was getting frustrated because she wanted to read the fillies a story from one of her favourite books, but all they wanted to do was play on the swings. She was watching them when she heard the voice again. "Look at them!" it whispered. "You know what's best for them and they didn't even listen. You're the *princess*, for Celestia's sake!"

She'd looked around but hadn't seen anyone who could have said it.

It was so odd. Ever since Gilda the Griffon planted the idea in her head that she shouldn't listen to her friends, Twilight had started to feel that everyone else's opinions were wrong. But was Gilda right?

Twilight decided to trot through the forest in the hope of clearing her head.

She was only alone for a few moments, however, before a loud crash signalled the presence of another, familiar pink pony.

"There you are!" Pinkie Pie shouted through the trees. "I have been looking aaaall over for you! I want to show you my awesome plan for the new kingdom's holiday celebrations!"

"Thanks, Pinkie. But now isn't a good time," Twilight said calmly. "I'm sort of busy."

"Okay! Will you be busy in ten minutes?" Pinkie asked, walking alongside her.

"Yes." Twilight was starting to get frustrated now. She wanted to be alone.

"Okay! What about in twenty minutes?!" Pinkie asked. To her, everything was a game.

"No! I'm busy now, I'm busy in ten minutes, and I'm busy in twenty minutes!" Twilight snapped. Her necklace began to dim, the colours churning. "Can't you see I don't have time to talk about your silly little parties?"

"What?" Pinkie Pie slumped to the

ground, hurt. "Sorry to bother you, Twilight. I was just trying to help. I'll leave you alone and go where someone wants me."

"Finally!" Twilight sneered. "That's the best idea you've had yet!" As she trotted off into the distance, Pinkie began to wonder what was really going on with Twilight Sparkle.

This time, she didn't think it was something a party could solve.

Chapter 9

A Head in the Clouds

Twilight Sparkle was planning to ask
Rainbow Dash if she'd seen Gilda the
Griffon. Even though the two of them were
no longer the best of friends, Rainbow saw
most of the comings and goings of the
residents of Ponyville. There were great
views of the town from up in the clouds.

Maybe talking to the griffon again would shed some light on the situation. There had to be more to what she tried to tell Twilight the other night after she crashed the secret meeting.

Rainbow Dash was sitting on a cloud high in the sky. She appeared to be arguing with a large group of Pegasi. She didn't hear Twilight trying to call her from below. "Good thing I have wings now," Twilight thought, taking off. She enjoyed the rush of cool air as she soared into the sky. It was fun to be an Alicorn!

"I have herded more clouds today than all you slowcoaches put together!" Rainbow Dash shouted at the other Pegasi.

"If you're so good, Rainbow Crash, why don't you help out the rest of us?" a big stallion named Hoops shouted back.

"Rainbow!" Twilight called out, but Rainbow didn't notice.

"You asked for it!" Rainbow shot back at Hoops, and took off into a showy barrel roll. She gathered a nearby cloud, combined it with two others, and then jumped onto it. A heavy flood of rain poured out of the bottom like a waterfall.

"Just call me Commander Hurricane!" Rainbow yelled, grinning from ear to ear.

"Rainbow Dash!" Twilight yelled a little louder. Why wasn't Rainbow listening? A princess was trying to speak to her! Twilight frowned. "Rainbow!"

Rainbow Dash finally noticed her friend hovering there. "Oh, hey, Twilight! Are you here to talk about my awesome plans for the new royal guard?"

"No." Twilight rolled her eyes like answering Rainbow's question was really hard work. "Have you seen Gilda?"

Twilight was acting really weird, and the colours on her necklace were swirling around.

"Are you okay?" Rainbow asked.

"Of course I am! Now, have you seen Gilda or not?"

"I think she's down by the farm with Trixie," Rainbow said. "Those two have been spending a lot of time together lately. If you ask me, it smells like trouble. Mixing pranks and magic is a bad idea, right?"

But Twilight didn't reply. She was already flying towards Sweet Apple Acres. She didn't even say "thank you".

CHAPTER 10

Drinking the Lily-Pad Slime

A good patch of leafy foliage was always ideal for spying. That was why Twilight Sparkle often found herself hiding behind trees and peering through hedges while doing various sorts of field research.

Today, Twilight crouched low behind a bush near the barn at Sweet Apple Acres.

She had spent the last ten minutes watching as Gilda and Trixie rolled a barrel of fresh apple juice from the stores and dumped it onto the grass. *Glug, glug, glug.* The juice spilled out quickly. Why anyone would waste it was beyond Twilight. Yet the two of them sniggered as they filled the empty barrel with gloopy green gunk that resembled the lily-pad slime from Froggy Bottom Bog.

"The ponies will never know what's hit 'em!" Gilda laughed. "This might be one of my greatest pranks yet!"

Trixie joined in. "And once the unlucky ponies who get a cup of 'juice' from this barrel take a sip, I'll swoop in and perform a magnificent spell to save them from the horrible taste!" she cackled.

"Personally, I think it's funnier not to

save them ... but whatever
you want, Trix!" Gilda
said. The two of
them high-fived.

"Hey!" Twilight
shouted. "You two!"

Gilda and Trixie
scrambled to cover up the barrel,
stepping in front of it to create a shield.
They looked around but didn't see
anyone until Twilight climbed out from
behind the bush. A couple of twigs were
still stuck in her mane.

"What are you, the undercover juice
police?" Gilda sneered. "Do you take all
your orders from Applejack now? Or are
you finally giving some orders of your
own, like a real royal pony, eh?"

Twilight was a little bit offended. "Well,
if you *must* know, I couldn't care less

what you do with that apple juice," she said, even though she knew she would definitely tell Granny Smith which barrel was filled with slime later. "But ... I wanted to ask you about..." she couldn't seem to find the words to ask Gilda for help.

Trixie tapped her hoof on the grass impatiently. She was still wearing her purple magician's robe and pointy hat covered in stars. "The Great and Powerful Trixie doesn't have all day, Twilight!" She was clearly still a little bitter about the time Twilight accidentally revealed her to be a fraud in front of all of Ponyville. Trixie probably didn't feel so "Great and Powerful" after that.

"What were you talking about the other night at my cottage?" Twilight asked Gilda.

The griffon shrugged casually. "I was just saying that if *I* were a princess, no one would be allowed to tell *me* what to do." Gilda put her claw on Twilight's shoulder and dug in a little too sharply. "What is it that *you* want to do, Twilight?"

"I want to . . ." Twilight hesitated. It felt strange to be asking for Gilda's opinion on the matter. But she *was* right. Why was she spending time and energy listening to her friends, when she herself knew exactly where to find the answers – the one place she always felt completely at ease, no matter where in Equestria she was? "I want to go to the library! The Crystal Empire Library!"

Gilda nodded in satisfaction. "I'll admit – the library thing is a little weird. But the Crystal Empire sounds awesome! You know what's best, Princess Twilight!"

A moment later, Twilight's jewelled necklace began to cloud and darken even more. Twilight didn't notice.

But there was definitely a new determination in her eyes. And it was a little scary.

✶ ✶ ✶

All that Twilight could think about now was that huge library in the Crystal Empire. It held hundreds of old books! There was no way the spell wasn't hidden in the pages of one of them.

"Thanks for your help," Twilight told Gilda and Trixie. "I have to go to the Crystal Empire now!" She spread her wings and took off into the air.

"That sounds so totally awesome! I'm coming, too," Gilda said, flying alongside her. "Is everything really made of crystals? What are the ponies like there?" Gilda began to imagine all the innocent victims whom she could play her pranks on.

"Trixie will go with you, too!" Trixie exclaimed. She pictured a whole new city of ponies who had never seen her "Great and Powerful" magic act.

Gilda and Trixie followed as Twilight soared through the air, winding through Ponyville and unaware of everything in her path. Fluttershy, who was leading a line of baby ducklings back to their mother at the pond, noticed Twilight approaching. "Hi, Twilight!" she said. She smiled and waved. "I'm so glad you're here! I came up with some new ideas for the baby-animal sanctuary that I wanted to share with you..."

But Twilight didn't even see. Fluttershy's pretty pink mane blew out from the gust of wind Twilight's wings created. Rarity watched in pure shock. Who was this pony and what had she done with their best friend, Twilight Sparkle? Twilight always stopped to talk to her friends. Then Rarity noticed that the Cosmic Spectrum gem on Twilight's necklace had lost some of its shine. This was a bad sign.

"Oh, Fluttershy!" Rarity said, trotting up to her. She was carrying a large sketchbook in her pack. It was full of new outfit designs she had been drawing for Twilight's imaginary kingdom. Even though she'd been annoyed after the meeting, she still wanted to help.

"Do you think she heard me?" Fluttershy squeaked sadly. "Twilight would never ignore someone like that on purpose, would she?"

But before Rarity could mention the necklace, Gilda the Griffon called out to them. "Twilight is a princess now, you guys! She's off to the Crystal Empire and doesn't need a bunch of silly Ponyville friends like you. She told me so herself. " Then she took off into the sky after Twilight.

Rarity and Fluttershy exchanged a worried look. "We'd better go and find Spike," Rarity said, looking to the sky. "He'll know what to do."

CHAPTER 11

Rallying the Hoofs

The lights were on inside Golden Oak Library, but Rarity and Fluttershy had knocked on the door three times and got no answer. "Is anyone at home?" Fluttershy whispered.

Rarity scoffed. "You're never going to get his attention like that! Watch and learn, darling." She cleared her throat. "Spiiiiike! Are you theeeeere?" Rarity trilled.

Spike flung open the door. "Hi, Rarity!"

Fluttershy wasn't offended that Spike hadn't greeted her. Everyone knew Spike had a major crush on Rarity. He was holding a large tub of ice cream and looked like he'd been crying.

"Are you okay?" Fluttershy asked.

"Twilight left me behind again!" Spike wailed. "She went back to the Crystal Empire and didn't even tell me! I had to hear it from Cranky Doodle Donkey.

"Unfortunately, it's true," Rarity said, entering the cottage. "We saw her leave."

"No goodbye or anything," added

Fluttershy. "Just whoosh! And gone."

"I think we can all agree that Twilight has not been herself today," Rarity said. "And I think that necklace is to blame!"

"Huh?" Spike and Fluttershy were confused.

"Last night I was trying to explain that although Cosmic Spectrum is beautiful, it can be dangerous if it is exposed to too many negative feelings. It absorbs them and makes the pony wearing it feel worse!"

"Poor Twilight," said Fluttershy.

"I knew it wasn't her fault!" Spike said. "We have to go and save Twilight. Together?"

"Together!" shouted Rarity and Fluttershy. Now all they had to do was find their friends and explain to them what had happened.

Chapter 12

Crystal Clear

"Look, I don't care what you do," Twilight snapped at Gilda and Trixie. "Just don't make any trouble!"

Twilight was almost at the Crystal Empire Library when she ran into Shining Armour. "Twily? I thought you were in Ponyville!"

"I was, but now I'm back again!" Twilight said, shifting from hoof to hoof anxiously. She was itching to look through those books.

"You must have lunch with me and Cadance in the castle," Shining Armour said.

"That's sounds nice, but I don't have time – maybe tomorrow. Talk to you later!" Twilight said, cantering past him.

He watched in confusion as she ran off. Normally, she was excited to see him. It was odd behaviour, especially for Twilight...

Shining Armour took off towards the castle. He had to find his wife, and fast!

It was a familiar scene for Twilight, sitting in an accidental fort made up of large, glittery books. She hungrily flipped through the pages of one called *Ancient Spells of the Crystal Empire: Volume Four.* The Crystal Heart Spell just had to be in there somewhere!

"Twilight! Are you in here?" Princess Cadance called out. Shining Armour had come to her after seeing his sister act so oddly. Something wasn't right, and he knew Cadance could help.

"Yes, I'm in here," Twilight sighed loudly from inside her book fort. She didn't want to see Cadance right now.

"Oh dear, Twilight…" Cadance shook her head. "It's just as I suspected."

"What is?" Twilight whined. "Me being as big a failure as I am? A pony with no leadership skills whatsoever?" Twilight hung her head in defeat.

"No, no, no. You're not a failure," Cadance said. She pointed her hoof at Twilight's neck. The Cosmic Spectrum wasn't shining at all any more. "Look! You've got so down on yourself and others that the necklace is magnifying your negative feelings!"

The young princess looked down at the gem, stunned. "I didn't even notice that it had changed." Twilight thought of all her friends back in Ponyville. Rarity had tried to warn her about the gemstone, but Twilight had been so distracted trying to find the spell that she hadn't listened.

Actually, Twilight had dismissed all of their ideas. She thought of Pinkie Pie's cake day, Applejack's family dinner time, Rainbow Dash's Pegasus royal guard,

Fluttershy's baby-animal sanctuary, and Rarity's kingdom fashions. The ideas didn't seem so bad now. Her friends were only trying to help. And how did she thank them? By ignoring them.

"Oh, Cadance, I've been so horrible to my friends!" Twilight said, standing up. Several nearby books toppled over like a set of building blocks. The necklace began to glow dimly. "I have to find them right now and apologise!"

Princess Cadance watched her gallop out of the library. Twilight was on the right track again.

Chapter 13

PFF to the Rescue

"Where do you think she'll be?"
Applejack said as the five ponies and their
baby-dragon companion made their way
through the gates of the Crystal Empire.
The last time they'd all visited was during
the Crystal Faire. Everything looked just
as pretty and shiny as it had before.

Rarity sighed. "Why am I not a Crystal pony?" she said, remembering how her coat had become temporarily glittery when they'd recovered the Crystal Heart. Unfortunately, the effects had worn off.

"What's that?!" said Pinkie Pie, pointing to a large crowd of Crystal ponies gathered near the fountain. "Whatever it is, it looks like fun! I'm gonna go see!"

All of a sudden, a bright flash of white illuminated the sky. *Pop!* A loud noise rang out. "Come on, everyone!" Applejack shouted, leading the way.

Applejack shoved her way to the front. A red-and-white-striped tent was set up.

Posters hung on the sides, praising the talents of THE GREAT AND POWERFUL TRIXIE, MAGICIAN EXTRAORDINAIRE. Gilda the Griffon stood outside the tent. "Step right up, Crystal ponies!" Gilda shouted. "Get yer tickets now! Step right up to see Equestria's most talented Unicorn – the Great and Powerful Trixie! Only three bits each!"

A yellow pony with a golden mane handed Gilda her money and entered the tent. Pinkie Pie looked around excitedly. "Oooooh! Does anyone have three bits I can borrow?!"

"Don't they know it's a scam?" Rainbow Dash said in disbelief.

Gilda continued on, unaware that the

Ponyville crew was standing in the crowd. "Trixie is so powerful that she once defeated an ursa major – all by herself!"

A couple more Crystal ponies paid Gilda and entered the tent.

"Hey, that's not true!" said Fluttershy. "It was Twilight who did that. Well, she took care of an ursa minor, anyway."

"I can't stand by and watch this any more," Applejack said. She trotted to the front and hopped up onto another crate. "Crystal ponies! Do not pay to see this show! This griffon and Unicorn are con-ponies who are trying to steal your bits!"

A low murmur broke out through the crowd.

"What are you doing here?!" Gilda spread her wings and screeched. "First you don't know how to take a hint when

Princess Twilight wants to get rid of you! And now you are ruining our show?

Trixie peeked out of the tent to see what was going on. The Crystal ponies all watched the scene with their jaws open. This was more of a show than they'd bargained for!

"No one wants you guys here!" Gilda yelled.

"That's not true!" A voice pierced through the crowd and interrupted the argument. "They are my best friends, and *I* want them here!" Twilight trotted over to her friends.

"What are you guys doing here?" Twilight asked.

"We came to rescue you, silly!" Pinkie Pie said matter-of-factly.

"I told them all about the necklace," Rarity explained. "We knew that you weren't being yourself."

"The Twilight we know would never be mean to her friends!" Fluttershy said.

"Or ditch us for those two!" Rainbow Dash added, motioning to Gilda and Trixie.

"I'm so sorry, you guys! I thought that listening to my own heart meant choosing whatever things *I* wanted in the kingdom." Twilight smiled, and the necklace began to glow. "Now I know that a princess is not defined by the things she chooses for her kingdom. All that matters is how she treats other ponies, especially her friends." She pulled them into a group hug. "Princess or not – we are all equal ponies!"

"Oh my, Twilight!" Rarity squealed. "Look at your necklace!"

Sure enough, the gem began to glow brighter than ever before. The light was low and pulsating, like a true beating heart. Nearby, the Crystal Heart grew brighter as well. It was almost as if the two jewels were linked by some invisible force. The ponies watched in awe as a gigantic, glittery rainbow suddenly burst forth from the centre of the Crystal Heart. It arched directly into Twilight's necklace!

"Ooooooh…" all the ponies cooed.

"Hey, look at that!" Rainbow shouted. "There are words on the Crystal Heart!"

Twilight knew it right away. The

Crystal Heart Spell had finally revealed itself to her. She trotted over and admired the words, which were lit up in shimmery gold. She took a deep breath and began to read them aloud:

"Friendship is the creed.
It has been from the start!
It's the only way to lead –
with your Crystal Heart!"

Twilight's coat sparkled as the spell took its effect on her. *Of course!* she thought as she read the words. Friendship had always been the answer to her problems. Why did she think it would be any different once she became a princess? Twilight looked around at the crowd of Crystal ponies cheering her on, her best friends standing next to her, and her brother and Cadance looking proud.

Twilight finally felt like a real princess.

✷ ✷ ✷

"Happy Cake Day, everyone!" Pinkie Pie shouted with glee, skipping through the centre of Ponyville. Since returning from the Crystal Empire, Twilight had started using all of her friends' suggestions as practice for being a real leader someday. Everywhere Princess Twilight looked, pony families were enjoying Crystal berry cupcakes and pies together. "Happy Cake Day!" they said to one another happily.

The Cutie Mark Crusaders had even

made a banner that read PONYVILLE CAKE DAY! and hung it across the front of the town hall. "Great idea, Princess Twilight!" Mr Cake shouted from the treat cart. "These things are selling like hotcakes!"

"They are hotcakes, dear," Mrs Cake laughed.

"Don't thank me!" Twilight said, walking over to where her friends sat on the grass. "Thank Pinkie Pie! She has the best ideas!"

Twilight took a bite of her cupcake, careful not to let her tiara fall off her head. Wearing it still took some getting used to, but everyone really liked it when she did. "In fact, *all* my friends have the best ideas."

Rarity smiled and winked at her. "So do you, *Princess* Twilight. So do you!"

Turn the page for a special surprise from Twilight Sparkle!

Dear reader,

I put together these bonus pages just for you! Have fun filling them in and sharing them with your friends!

Your friend,
Twilight Sparkle

The Write Stuff

When Twilight came to live in Ponyville, the beautiful and wise Princess Celestia asked for letters about the lessons Twilight was learning as she studied the magic of friendship. Use the space below to write your own letter to Princess Celestia and tell her all about your friends!

Dear Princess Celestia,

My friends are called _____ _____.

Some fun activities we like to do together are _____, _____ and _____.

Our favourite film to watch together is _____.

The best part about friendship is _____!

I would also like to tell you that _____ _____.

Your faithful student,

_____

Make Your Mark

When ponies discover what makes them special, they earn their unique cutie mark! What sorts of things do you like to do that make you feel special? What do your friends like to do? List them below and design your own cutie marks!

Name	Hobbies	Favourite Colours	Cutie Mark
Twilight Sparkle	Magic, reading, stargazing	Purple, pink	
Fluttershy	Caring for animals	Pink, yellow	
_____ *(write your name here)*			
_____ *(insert your friend's name)*			
_____ *(insert your friend's name)*			

Cast a Spell

As a student of magic, Twilight Sparkle has to learn lots of spells for different purposes. Unfortunately, there isn't a spell for everything. If you could recite a magic spell, what would it do? Write your own spell here.

Name of spell _____

Created by _____

Purpose _____

This spell is: *(circle one from each set)*

silly   fun   serious

easy   medium   difficult

It must be spoken in this type of voice:

(circle one)

soft   regular   loud   extra loud

This spell must be repeated _____ times.

Write your spell here:

_____

_____

_____

_____

At a Loss for Words

Twilight has misplaced some of the words for her spell! Help her by finding and circling the words below.

P	R	I	N	C	E	S	S	P
S	C	N	Y	H	P	P	O	R
U	R	W	G	I	E	N	E	Q
T	Y	L	K	L	Y	A	A	H
N	S	E	L	V	D	L	R	S
C	T	W	I	L	I	G	H	T
A	A	L	H	L	P	Y	V	U
K	L	I	B	R	A	R	Y	D
E	F	T	I	A	R	A	Y	Y

TIARA   CAKE   TWILIGHT
SPIKE   SPELL   READ
PONYVILLE   CRYSTAL   PRINCESS
LIBRARY   STUDY   HEART

Book Stars

Twilight Sparkle loves to read so much that she lives in a library! Use the space below to list all the books you read. Each time you finish reading a book, give it a score of one star to four stars. Four stars mean you loved it!

Twilight Sparkle and the Crystal Heart Spell ★★★★

Friendly Advice

When Twilight Sparkle is stuck on a difficult problem, she likes to ask Princess Cadance for advice because her friend always has something wise to say. Whom do you go to for help? Why? Use the space below to talk about someone who offers help when you need it most. He or she might be a friend, a relative or a teacher!

_____

_____

_____

_____

_____

_____

_____

_____

A Daring Do Adventure

Studying is fun, but Twilight also loves to get lost in a good novel – especially stories about Daring Do, the fearless pony who goes on all sorts of exciting adventures through jungles and forbidden temples. Use these pages to write your own adventure starring Daring Do. Don't forget to include some daunting obstacles for Daring to overcome!

Once upon a time, Daring Do was…

_____

_____

_____

_____

_____

_____

_____

_____

_____

_____

_____

_____

_____

_____

_____

_____

_____

The End!

Wear It Well

Twilight Sparkle is overjoyed when Princess Cadance gives her a beautiful heart necklace. What is your favourite thing to wear? What makes it so special? Describe it and draw a picture of it here!

Pony Scramble

The enchantment on Twilight's new necklace made her feel all mixed up! It took the help of her best friends to help put things straight again. Unscramble their names below!

1. ARNBWIO SHDA

    _ _ _ _ _ _ _   _ _ _ _

2. CJPKLEPAA

    _ _ _ _ _ _ _ _ _

3. YIARRT

    _ _ _ _ _ _

4. YTHUFLSERT

    _ _ _ _ _ _ _ _ _ _

5. PSKIE

    _ _ _ _ _

6. IEPIKN IEP

    _ _ _ _ _ _   _ _ _

Answers: 1. Rainbow Dash,
2. Applejack, 3. Rarity, 4. Fluttershy,
5. Spike, 6. Pinkie Pie

Pony Trivia Time

Twilight has been living in Ponyville with her friends, but there are lots of other places in Equestria that she has visited. Use the clues provided to name some of them!

1. The Pegasus ponies reside in this cloud city high in the sky:

    _____

2. The big city where Applejack once spent time with Aunt and Uncle Orange:

    _____

3. The stunning capital city of Equestria, where Princess Celestia resides:

_____

4. This sparkling empire is Shining Armour and Cadance's home:

_____

5. The dark and mysterious forest where Zecora the Zebra spends her days:

_____